Maybe A BEAR Ate It!

Maybe A BEAR Ate It!

by ROBIE H. HARRIS

illustrated by MICHAEL EMBERLEY

SCHOLASTIC INC.
New York Toronto London Auckland Sydney
Mexico City New Delhi Hong Kong Buenos Aires

It's gone!

It's nowhere!

I can't find it anywhere!

Where — is — my book?

I need my book!

Maybe a  **BEAR**

ate it!

Maybe a

STEGOSAURUS

stomped on it!

Maybe a

RHINO

ran away with it!

Maybe a

BAT

flew high up in the sky

with it!

Maybe a **SHARK** swallowed it!

Maybe an ELEPHANT fell asleep on it!

Well — I can't go to sleep without it!

So I better go look for it!

Looking . . .

I'm looking . . .

I'm still looking . . .

Hey, look!
I found my book!

You know what?
I LOVE MY BOOK!

For Michael—
For your wonderful friendship and amazing art! – R.H.H.

For Kieran—
May you never lose anything special again. – M.E.

No part of this publication may be reproduced, stored in a retrieval system, or transmitted in any form or by any means, electronic, mechanical, photocopying, recording, or otherwise, without written permission of the publisher. For information regarding permission, write to Scholastic Inc., Attention: Permissions Department, 557 Broadway, New York, NY 10012. • This book was originally published by Orchard Books in 2008. • ISBN-13: 978-0-545-09918-9 ISBN-10: 0-545-09918-8 • Text copyright © 2008 by Bee Productions, Inc. Illustrations copyright © 2008 by Michael Emberley. All rights reserved. Published by Scholastic Inc. SCHOLASTIC and associated logos are trademarks and/or registered trademarks of Scholastic Inc. ORCHARD BOOKS and design are registered trademarks of Watts Publishing Group, Ltd., used under license.• 12 11 10 9 8 7 6 5 4 3 2 1   8 9 10 11 12 13/0

Printed in the U.S.A. 40 • This edition first printing, September 2008 • Book design by Alison Klapthor